Sundancer

A Mystical Fantasy

written and illustrated

by

EDWARD HAYS

OTHER BOOKS BY THE AUTHOR:
(available from Forest of Peace Books, Inc.)

Prayers for the Domestic Church
Prayers for the Servants of God
Secular Sanctity
Twelve and One-Half Keys
Pray All Ways

SUNDANCER   6/93

copyright © 1982, by Edward M. Hays

Library of Congress Catalog Card Number: 82-83135
ISBN 0-939516-04-7

published by
Forest of Peace Books, Inc.
Route One — Box 247
Easton, Kansas 66020

printed by
Hall Directory, Inc.
Topeka, Kansas 66608

October 1982

Forest of Peace Books, Inc.

dedicated

to

Steve Kongs

and

Sandi DeSalvo

October 23, 1982

SUNDANCER

ot that long ago . . .

yet once upon a time, there was a stately old house perched on a hilltop. Next to the house was a beautiful flower garden which looked out across a long green lawn that rolled down a hill to a narrow country lane. In the garden grew many lovely flowers, arranged neatly according to their height and their importance.

The aristocrats of the garden
were the roses
who were somewhat snobbish
and usually spoke
with refined British accents.
The asters,
being well educated,
delighted in discussing
philosophy and scholarly books.

The irises formed the security force of the flower bed and stood rigidly at attention with their long, slender, green-leafed swords at their sides. The vigilant irises made sure that all who lived in the flower bed obeyed the laws and regulations. The garden contained many other interesting and beautiful flowers; among them were the daisies. They were carefree and fun-loving, and their funny antics caused many of the little flowers to laugh. The timid violets and other little flowers lived in constant fear of offending the powerful irises or of falling out of favor with the even more authoritarian gladioli.

ow, one of the little flowers was unique with its brilliant yellow blossom. Even though it was short and grew close to the earth, this flower was as bright as the sun.

Although it belonged to the same family as the zinnia and the chrysanthemum, they, nevertheless, refused to acknowledge their cousin because it seemed so short and insignificant. The other flowers sometimes called the short yellow flower "runt." At other times, they called it "Frenchy" because it was an immigrant and had a strange sounding French name. But, you see, all the flowers in the garden were of immigrant stock. Their parents or grandparents had come to this land aboard the Mayflower or some later ship. The flower itself cared for neither of these nicknames, but preferred to be called "Sundancer."

Sundancer was particularly proud of its sun-like blossom and its smooth, tapered, straight-edged green leaves. But what most distinguished it was that while the other flowers were content to live in the flower bed, Sundancer dreamed of far-off and romantic places.

This free-spirited flower daydreamed of climbing towering snowcapped mountain peaks or of dancing in the surf of some exotic tropical island beach. Sundancer also imagined traveling to New York or Paris, or flying down to Rio.

Often Sundancer would share these dreams of distant places with the rest of the flowers, asking them, "Why do we have to live so confined inside these flower beds? Why can't we be free to roam around the lawn or to grow wherever we choose?"

At questions like these, the roses would only smile with a certain smug disdain, saying to themselves, "Who would *want* to live in such places?" The asters delighted in giving Sundancer lengthy answers concerning behavioral patterns and genetic conditioning. The other flowers would nod in agreement that living in a flower bed was only natural for "civilized" flowers.

But, the real reason why they refused to consider Sundancer's dreams was that each of them, from the shy pansies to the tough irises, were afraid. They were fearful of the world that existed beyond their well-ordered flower bed society.

Our would-be adventurer often warned the others, "We must be careful. We live in a flower bed, and those who spend all their time in bed are sick . . . and they die in bed!"

The asters responded, "People also make love in bed and that's what we're all about." The lilies, who were the devout churchgoers, clutched their black bibles all the tighter and shook their delicate heads at all this talk about sex in public. Sundancer answered the asters, "Yah, people make love in bed, but they don't spend their whole lives in bed!"

"Enough of this shouting; quiet, all of you," came the command of the sword-carrying irises. "The sun is setting and all decent flowers should be retiring."

All the flowers quickly obeyed, and silence, together with twilight, began to settle over the long green lawn and the beautiful flower garden.

None of the flowers admitted, even to themselves, that it was their fear of life outside the garden that was the reason they conformed to the strict laws of the garden. They were afraid to live on the other side of the gravel walkway that bordered the garden. They were afraid that wild beasts might eat them or that they might be stepped on and killed. Instead of admitting their fears, it was their custom to give little speeches about their importance to society: "Do we not give beauty and meaning to weddings and funerals? Do we not give happiness to lovers, and are we not a source of pleasure for all who see us?" But these and other boastings were only illusions to help them to hide their deadly fear of the world that existed beyond their small society fixed securely between the old house and the gravel walkway.

Slowly a great full moon rose in the east. The lawn and the garden were gently covered with pale, bluish light. Sundancer, feeling lonely and alienated, whispered a short prayer: "Lord, please help me to escape from this flower garden."

"It's possible, my friend," came a strange voice that Sundancer had never heard in the garden before. Looking about, the flower saw a large brown cricket on the edge of the gravel walkway. The cricket had an old leather knapsack on his back.

Sundancer was stunned. While having heard the songs of crickets before, never had one of them ever spoken to the yellow flower.

"I couldn't help but overhear your argument with the other flowers as well as your prayer about wanting to be free," said the cricket, his white hair and long beard glistening in the moonlight.

Overcoming surprise and bewilderment, Sundancer asked the unexpected visitor, "Are you a hearth cricket? Are you from our master's house?"

"Yes and no," replied the cricket, as he slipped off his leather knapsack and sat on it. "I mean about being from our Master's house. I am a field cricket, not a house cricket. There's a difference, you know!"

Sundancer looked down with fascination as the moonlight visitor continued, "As a field cricket, I've seen a lot of fields in a lot of places. I've traveled far and wide, to distant lands. Oh, but excuse me, I didn't catch your name."

"My name is Sundancer," replied the yellow flower.

"A perfect name for you," said the cricket. "My name is Tien-shan (*Tee-en' shawn*), which means 'celestial mountains.' Many years ago, while traveling northward from Tibet, I was crossing the Tien-shan mountains when in a moment of awe I realized that those things we call obstacles in life are in reality celestial mountains. I took the name to remind myself to pause and stand in wonder at life's problems instead of trying always to avoid them . . . which is impossible anyway. That's an insight that has been of great help to me as I worked at 10,000 odd jobs while traveling around the world. After hiring myself out as a fighting cricket in China, I traveled to Japan and lived a life of pure luxury in a tea house. The Japanese are definitely a refined and cultured people. They enjoyed my singing and gave me an ivory box in which to live. They believe that crickets bring good luck. How about you, Sundancer? Do you believe that our meeting is no accident and that I can bring you good luck?"

"Yes," whispered Sundancer, who
looked over quickly to see if the irises were asleep.
"I believe that somehow you are an answer
to my prayer about being free.
Yes, I believe you are good luck."

"Good, I'm glad you believe," chirped in the bearded cricket. "In my wild wanderings across this earth, I chanced upon sages, scholars and poets who opened doors within me to life's most ancient riddles. In the same way, I can help you to be free; that is, if you really want to be free."

"Oh, yes, yes," said Sundancer. "I want to be free more than anything else in this world. I long to dance, to live outside the safe but narrow, cramped confines of this garden. But all the other flowers say it's impossible. There are laws here, you know, laws that are supposed to be for the common good of all. And we have customs as well, and sometimes they are as rigid as the laws. Tell me, Tien-shan, do you know some mystical magic from Tibet with which I can escape from here?"

"No magic in this world can make you free, Sundancer," answered Tien-shan, "but if you are willing to learn and also willing to risk everything, I will help you to be free. I will return to you in one month, when the next full moon rises in the east. When I return I will give you your first lesson. But, until that night, I want you to repeat this simple prayer over and over. I learned it years ago from a house cricket who lived in a Hindu temple in Rishikesh, India.

"Listen well, for this is the prayer:

>Lord, from the unreal, lead me to the Real.
>From darkness, lead me to Light.
>From death, lead me to immortality.

When you pray it, close your eyes and sit very still. And believe — that's very important. Now, repeat it after me."

Sundancer, with eyes closed, repeated the prayer over and over. Upon opening them, Sundancer discovered that the cricket was nowhere to be seen.

*T*he days passed quickly as Sundancer awaited the next full moon. Taken up by the possibility of escape and so absorbed in the strange power of the little prayer, Sundancer no longer felt a need to argue with the other flowers. Yet, with eagerness growing for the first lesson, it seemed that the full moon would never come. But as it rose majestically over the horizon, Sundancer began to hear the song of the mysterious troubadour, Tien-shan.

Tien-shan was singing a song
about the edelweiss,
that charming flower
that roams freely among
the snow-peaked mountains.
Greeting Sundancer,
the cricket spoke,
"Good evening, my young student.
Ready for your first lesson?"

"Yes, very ready, Master Tien,"
responded Sundancer.

"Our first lesson," chirped Tien-shan, "deals with reality. If you wish to escape from your prison — your playpen of unreality — you must be willing to face the real world. Your first lesson is to learn how to lay aside the common use of glib or empty words."

Tien-shan paused to see if Sundancer was listening — and the flower was, with deep concentration.

The cricket continued, "Lay aside all those words and behavior you learned as a child to gain the approval of others or to appease them. Such habitual responses must go because they are part of playing a role. You must stop playing the role of a flower."

"Playing the role?" asked Sundancer.

"Yes," said Tien-shan, "you were created to be something more than a splash of color in some bridal bouquet or to end your life looking 'pretty,' standing politely in some ceramic vase. These are merely social roles, and you must avoid them because they imprison you. They prevent you from being you, from being free. Sundancer, you were not created for profit or practicality, to be picked or used. In Tibet, my friends told me that there are two unpardonable crimes: to abuse small children and to pick wild flowers!"

Sundancer nodded, "I understand, and I will try to do what you say."

"Good," said Tien-shan, "then continue to pray your prayer and to sit each day in silence. Until the next full moon . . . "

Without even a good-bye, Tien-shan disappeared. In the days and weeks that followed, Sundancer attempted to live the lesson of being truly oneself. The other little flowers in the garden only shook their heads with concern as Sundancer refused to be forced into the social roles required in a well-ordered flower garden. Bravely, Sundancer refused to absorb the frowns and hostile looks of the larger and stronger flowers who held power and authority over the garden.

Each night Sundancer watched the moon grow smaller and smaller. Then slowly it began to increase, growing larger and larger as it covered the garden with its milky light. Each day Sundancer sat in silence and prayed the prayer. And, with diligence, the little yellow flower practiced the lesson of the wise old cricket.

A full moon of great beauty graced the eastern
night sky as Tien-shan came whistling into the garden.

"Good evening, Sundancer," he said with a smile.

"Have you done your homework?"

"Yes. It was not easy, but I have been faithful to the lesson," answered Sundancer. "Is tonight's lesson easier?"

"No, my friend," said Tien-shan, "tonight's lesson is a most difficult one, but also most necessary if you wish to be free. Bend your head down here close to me." Sundancer leaned as close as possible to the cricket. Suddenly Tien-shan shouted in Sundancer's ear, "You are NOTHING!"

Sundancer jerked upright in a reflex-quick movement. The cricket continued in a normal tone, "You are but a tiny speck in an unbelievably enormous universe, which is itself but a tiny speck in a vast sea of cosmic galaxies. You, my friend, must overcome your need to be 'someone' and learn to be who you are. You must learn to embrace with love your littleness in the vast sweep of all creation. Such awareness is freedom and its name is humility. You must learn to face this reality without cheap cardboard defenses. You must stand and face this great terror without fear, confident that you are continuously embraced in a deep Divine love — even if you are so insignificant." Tien-shan, with staff in hand, silently slipped away from the garden.

Sundancer shivered at the thought of this task but repeated the prayer: "Lord, from the unreal, lead me to the Real. From darkness, lead me to Light. From death, lead me to immortality."

he days and weeks passed as the moon changed in shape, making its cycle from fullness to emptiness and back again toward fullness. As a brilliant moon — one night short of being full — captured the evening sky, Tien-shan entered unnoticed into the flower bed.

"Hello again, Sundancer," he said. "I am one night early this time, but with good reason. I hope you are ready for your final lesson, for you must now face death itself — the most ancient of all enemies. This is the oldest fear that imprisons young and old. Your task is not so much to learn to be brave, but rather it is to not fear death, to not fear growing old. You must learn to love that dark journey, to court death as a companion. Fear not the unknown pain of your death and the unchartered passageways of the mystery that lie beyond the dark, damp tomb."

"Master," answered Sundancer, "I have done that already. I sensed that this would be the next lesson. I have tried to live it, as well as the other lessons, this past month. Now, Master Tien, am I ready to escape? I have completed the three lessons, am I now ready to be re-born and be free?"

Tien-shan, his voice empty of music or song, answered Sundancer slowly, "Beware, my friend, do not be fooled by a satin-slick religious language. To be truly new, especially while facing the reality of your personal insignificance, is more painful than death itself."

Sundancer's heart pounded as the old cricket continued, "Many are the seekers who have chosen death, but how many of them truly have had the courage to be reborn? How many, Sundancer, have had the courage to experience a resurrection to a totally new life instead of simply settling for some modification of their former ways of living? Without such a painful rebirth, a new freedom becomes only another prison — a new and perhaps more comfortable cage to protect them from the crushing dread of reality."

Tien-shan paused and looked with affection into the eyes of Sundancer. Then he continued, "To see the world as it truly is — saturated with the sacred — is both wonderful and terrifying."

"Sundancer," he added softly, "if you wish to be free, then you must learn to live out at the very edge, the brink of life. Die to your desire for security, to your hunger for constant reassurances . . . live on the edge. Like reformed alcoholics, never take your freedom for granted. Each day, like them, practice the escape lessons you have learned. The sign of those who have truly escaped, of those who are truly free, is that they live in perpetual humility."

The wise old cricket, having finished the lesson, now raised the well-worn leather knapsack onto his shoulders. Sundancer looked with disbelief, "You're not leaving, are you? I need you now more than ever!"

Tien-shan adjusted a shoulder strap and answered, "Yes, my friend, it is time for me to leave. Every good teacher works his or her way out of a job — that is if they're really good teachers. You know all you need to know. Now you must be free, even of me. Don't worry, here in our hearts we will always be united. A special bond links those who share the truth, and even death cannot break such a bond. The boundaries of space and time are removed easily by those who have found true freedom — which is love."

And he was gone. Sundancer knew that he would never return again. The small yellow flower knew what he had to do. Suddenly, a chilling night breeze blew across the flower garden. The sleeping flowers wrapped themselves more securely in their green leafy blankets and Sundancer shivered.

All that night,
as the moon slowly crossed the night sky,
Sundancer prayed in the garden.
As the others slept on in peaceful dreams,
Sundancer wrestled with
fear and death.

T he next morning, Sundancer stood before all the flowers and announced boldly: "I am leaving the garden!"

The daisies and marigolds pleaded with the little yellow flower to reconsider . . . encouraging it to make the necessary compromises. Meanwhile, the other flowers held official council about what should be done with this little upstart.

The asters spoke of the domino effect, that soon others would also want to leave. "What would the master of the house do then? We would all suffer," replied the roses. Finally, the council reached a firm decision. Sundancer, like all the other flowers, would have to obey the rules and customs of the garden. This unanimous decision was announced to all the flowers. Most of them voiced agreement or nodded consent. Sundancer listened in silence but said nothing.

That night all the flowers slept in peace, thankful that this troubling issue had been finally resolved by those who "knew best."

At midnight, when the full moon was halfway in her course, a loud shout awakened all the flowers: "ALARM, ALARM . . . Sundancer is escaping from the garden!"

The irises, with drawn swords and flickering lanterns, apprehended Sundancer in the middle of the gravel walkway that bordered the flower bed. Brought before the High Council of the Flowers, Sundancer's trial lasted but a short while. The sentence of the court was as follows:

"For refusing to obey the laws
of this garden,
for endangering the common good
of all the flowers,
you, Sundancer, are hereby sentenced
to forty lashes of the whip.
May your punishment be a teacher
and medicine for you."

The High Council's sentence was carried out the following day. Sundancer's punishment was painful, the tip of the whip tearing into the flower's long, slender leaves. As blow followed blow, the once straight and beautiful leaves became jagged . . . ripped by the repeated slashes of the whip.

On the next to last blow of the whip, quite by accident, the end of the whip caught the slender stem that supported Sundancer's beautiful golden head. The stem snapped . . . and with a cry of agonizing pain, the yellow head fell limp.

Without even a hint of remorse, the court ordered the dead body of Sundancer to be removed . . . to be thrown outside the garden where it might be visible to all.

So the irises carried the limp body, bruised and beaten, to the edge of the garden and tossed it out onto the barren gravel walkway.

The once beautiful, yellow blossomed head now lay twisted beneath the crumpled, jagged and torn leaves. The rest of that day, the other flowers looked down at the dead body of Sundancer.

Among all the flowers,
not a single discussion was heard about freedom
or about living another life that was outside
the boundaries of the flower garden.
Sundancer's punishment and death had not
  been wasted —
the lesson was clear to one and to all.

With sunrise, on the next day, the flowers were surprised to see that Sundancer had disappeared. The body of the dead yellow flower was nowhere to be seen.

Speculation spread through the garden. Some of the flowers said that the crickets had come by night and taken the body away. It had for some time been rumored that the dead yellow flower was a close friend of the crickets. Still others among the flowers maintained that the gardener had removed the body. Some of the marigolds, who had been friends of the dead Sundancer, recalled that when alive the yellow flower had spoken about a journey to some "center."

Other flowers agreed: "Yes, Sundancer had spoken about finding some inner passageway to a place where all power lies, where all truth is known."

Even the daisies, usually given only to laughter and humor, were eager to help solve the mystery. One of them told the group, "Yes, that's right. While alive, Sundancer once quoted to us the lines of the poet Robert Frost. We couldn't make heads or tails of the riddle, however. What do you think it means?

> We sit around in a ring and suppose,
> but the Secret sits in the middle
> and knows."

And so as all the flowers went to sleep that night, some were fearful that they might do something wrong and be punished as was Sundancer. Others fell asleep sad, for they missed their happy yellow-headed friend.

At sunrise, on the third day,
the flowers awoke to a shining surprise.
In the middle of the well-manicured,
long, sloping green lawn
was a beautiful yellow flower . . .
a short yellow flower
which sparkled with the splendor of the sun.
Strangely enough, the long leaves
were jagged and torn,
like those of the dead Sundancer.

But this flower was not dead.
On the contrary, it was alive —
very much alive.

And soon, other yellow, sun-like flowers
appeared here and there
in the front lawn.
They also appeared along the roadside,
in fields and meadows across the road.
They grew along the railroad tracks,
they grew in the lawns of the very rich
and beside the rickety shacks of the poor.
They grew in cities
and in the country.
They grew, it became apparent,
wherever they wished.
Unlike the other flowers
who always lived in the flower beds,
these brilliant yellow-headed little flowers
now traveled freely everywhere.
All attempts to force them back
into the rigid life of the flower beds failed.

They had become free.

And when it comes time for them to die —
as all that lives must die —
unlike other flowers
whose blossoms fade and wither,
these flowers of the sun
mysteriously bloom again
in their last hour.
As they die,
they bloom into beautiful white globes . . .
luminous, airy and mystical
like the full moon,
and pregnant with power.

At the very moment of their death,
in a silky silent explosion,
multitudes of white parachutes
are released.
Each parachute carries beneath it
a single sacred message: freedom is life.

The four winds
gently carry
these white messengers
to the furthermost corners
of the earth, to all nations and to all peoples.

But, as is usually the case,
those who are liberated
in a world of slaves
are judged by that world
as obnoxious.

They are judged to be pests.

These pests, the freed ones,
only upset the well-manicured lawns
of the routines of daily life.
By their very presence among us
they constantly challenge
our lack of freedom,
and so, as a defense,
they are classified as offensive,
repugnant and worthless.

They are called . . .
Dandelions
(from the French, dent de lion: lion's tooth).

They are called weeds.

While rejected by the world,
these Sundancers
sing a song,
like that of Tien-shan,
the wise old cricket:

"Let those with ears hear
and those with eyes see."

"To die

but not to perish

is to be

eternally present."

Tao Te Ching

Unless a grain of wheat falls to the earth and dies, it remains just a grain of wheat. But if it dies, it produces much fruit.

— Jesus from John's Gospel: Christianity

The souls of the just are in the hand of God . . . . They seemed, in the view of the foolish, to be dead; and their passing away . . . utter destruction . . . . If before others, indeed, they be punished, yet is their hope full of immortality . . . they shall shine and dart about as sparks.

— Book of Wisdom: Judaism

If slayers think that they kill, and if the slain think that they die, they know not the ways of truth. The Eternal in each person cannot kill; the Eternal in each person cannot die.

When all the knots of the heart have been released, then truly a mortal becomes immortal.

— Upanishads: Hinduism

Few cross over the river. Most are stranded on this side . . . . But the wise, following the way, cross over, beyond the reach of death. They leave the dark way for the way of light. They leave home, seeking happiness on the hard road . . . . Rejoicing greatly in their freedom, in this world the wise become light: pure, shining, free.

— The Dhammapada: Buddhism

Man is asleep; when he dies he wakes up.

Prophet Mohammed: Islam

Never fear your journey ahead, for as God has watched over you all your life . . . so He will take you through the darkest vale, into the light.

— White Eagle: American Indian

author

As an author, Edward Hays' numerous books reflect the many other facets of his life . . . as a Catholic priest, as director of a contemplative community (Shantivanam), as an artist, a storyteller, spiritual director and movie enthusiast.

With his father having had a great love of flowers, the author grew up in the Midwest surrounded by their beauty. In his late twenties, he became fascinated with the concept of death — including his own. He subsequently wrote and directed a film on the theme of death, *A Time To Die*, and this book is a further reflection of his interest in that mystery.

Sundancer, as well as his other stories and parables, will hopefully be a doorway through which his readers may discover the mystical contained within the ordinary.

acknowledgements

While a single name appears on the cover as the book's author, no one person is ever the sole author of a book. Rather than a single influence, a book is a communion of countless sources: co-workers, friends, teachers and other authors who have over many years inspired the writer. These persons also deserve to be acknowledged.

With gratitude, I acknowledge the unseen work of Thomas Turkle who directed this publication. He and Thomas Skorupa also worked in concert in the editing of the manuscript.

Thanks to David DeRusseau for his work on the original lettering for the title, his layout design and his numerous artistic recommendations.

I appreciate the supportive counsel of two co-workers, Jennifer Sullivan and Joanne Meyer; along with the encouragement of Greg Bien and numerous other friends.

I wish to also recognize the support and creative advice of Bob and Ann Nunley while the manuscript was in its early stages. I express my gratitude to Ernest Becker, author of *The Denial of Death*, who spoke so insightfully of the mystery of death.

And finally, my thanks to the printers, Steve and Cliff Hall of Hall Directory, Inc., who from a professional position assisted in the overcoming of technical difficulties. To them, to all their employees who helped to creatively print it, and to all those unnamed "others" . . . Thank You!